Enough is enough!

"That must be Lardy Lorraine's picture!" whispered Joshua Barton. His whisper was loud enough for everyone in the class to hear.

That was enough for Alex. Joshua Barton had gone too far today! Without thinking, Alex picked up a giant sponge that was lying on her table. It was wet and gooey from wiping up many spills. Taking aim, Alex flung the sponge at Joshua. BLAP! It hit the side of his face.

"Yeeaack!" Joshua yelled.

"Who threw the sponge at Joshua?" Mrs. Feather asked.

Alex stiffened. The class became silent. . . .

The ALEX Series

by Nancy Simpson

• Shoelaces and Brussels Sprouts
• French Fry Forgiveness
• Hot Chocolate Friendship
• Peanut Butter and Jelly Secrets
• Mint Cookie Miracles
• Cherry Cola Champions
• The Salty Scarecrow Solution
• Peach Pit Popularity
• T-Bone Trouble
• Apple Turnover Treasure
• Crocodile Meatloaf

Cherry Cola Champions

Nancy Simpson

Cook
Communications

Cook Communications, Colorado Springs, Colorado 80918
Cook Communications, Paris, Ontario
Kingsway Communications, Eastbourne, England

CHERRY COLA CHAMPIONS

Cover design by Megan Keane DeSantis and Dana Sherrer
Cover illustration by Don Stewart

First printing, 1988
Printed in the United States of America
04 03 02 01 00 11 10 9 8 7

Library of Congress Cataloging-in-Publication Data
Levene, Nancy S., 1949-
Cherry Cola Champions.
Summary: Disgruntled at first when a slow, fat girl is put on the fourth grade soccer team, Alex makes a decision to help her improve, a project which pays off for everyone concerned.
[1. Christian life—Fiction. 2. Soccer—Fiction] I. Dorenkamp, Michelle, ill. II. Title.
PZ7.L5724Ch 1988
[Fic] 88-12294
ISBN: 0-78143-372-X

To Jesus, my shield and anchor
and
To my daughter, Cara,
a mighty champion in the Lord
and a precious gift to me.

When God's children are in need,
you be the one to help them out.

Romans 12:13
The Living Bible

ACKNOWEDGMENTS

Thank you, Mom and Dad, for the computer, and thank you, Ed Marquette, for your many suggestions and wonderful creativity, especially regarding garbage disposals! Thank you, Cara, for being involved in every aspect of this book.

CONTENTS

CHAPTER 1

Lardy Lorraine

The ball flew through the air, spinning toward Alex. Leaping in the air, she met the ball and neatly directed it to the ground with her right knee.

"What a trap!" somebody roared from the sidelines.

Ignoring the cheers, Alex easily dribbled the ball downfield, now dodging to the right, now twisting to the left. No defender could catch her. Moving to the goal, Alex paused threateningly in front of the goalkeeper. Suddenly, Alex slammed the ball with her right foot. BAM! The ball shot past the keeper. The referee raised his hands. GOAL! The crowd went wild.

"Alex!" called a voice next to her ear. "Are you listening to me?"

Alex jerked herself out of the daydream and gazed at her friend, Janie. "Huh?" she asked.

Janie narrowed her eyes in frustration. "I said, 'I wonder what Ms. Springate is going to have us do in gym today.' "

"I hope it's soccer!" Alex answered quickly. Her eyes sparkled as she remembered the imaginary goal she had just made.

"Alex! You are hopeless," Janie sighed. "No matter what we do in gym, you like it."

Janie was right. Alex loved gym class because Alex loved sports. And she liked gym class this year more than ever before because Ms. Springate was Kingswood Elementary's new gym teacher. Alex thought Ms. Springate was wonderful. For one thing, Ms. Springate had convinced the other teachers to let their classes take running breaks every morning. That meant that Alex and the rest of the children got to run as many laps as they could around the playground in ten minutes. The idea was to see how many miles each child could run.

Alex had already run nine miles and had nine stars by her name on the chart that hung in the fourth-grade classroom. She was tied for first place with Joshua Barton. He also had nine stars. Alex frowned when she thought of Joshua Barton. He was such a show-off!

"Come on, children," Ms. Springate called. "We want to get in a full game of soccer. I have chosen the teams. Joshua will be the captain of one team and Alex will be the other captain."

Alex grinned with pleasure. She was beginning to like soccer almost as much as softball.

Ms. Springate called out the names of each team's players. Alex was thankful to see Aaron join her team. Aaron was the best goalkeeper in the fourth grade. She was also happy that her best friend, Janie, was on her team.

Alex gritted her teeth when Zachary Logan was called to be on Joshua's team. She had wanted Zack on her team. He was a fantastic dribbler. He and Alex got along well together as forwards. Joshua gave Alex an irritating grin.

One by one, Ms. Springate called out the names. Finally, everyone had joined a team except one girl.

"Lardy Lorraine," the boys snickered.

Lorraine ducked her head and stared, red faced, at the floor. Alex held her breath. She hoped that Lorraine was not on her team. Lorraine was too fat and too slow to play soccer.

"Lorraine, you are on Alex's team," Ms. Springate said.

Low cheers and giggles sounded from Joshua Barton's team.

Keeping her head bent low, Lorraine shuffled over to where Alex's team was standing.

"We will keep the same teams for the entire soccer season," Ms. Springate told the children. "Now, let's play soccer!"

"A disaster! It was a total disaster!" Alex complained to her friends at lunch.

Janie and Julie looked at each other and began laughing.

"What's so funny?" demanded Alex.

"Now, Alex," Janie tried her best to stop giggling. "You have to admit it was funny."

"Especially when Lorraine fell over backwards and Joshua fell on top of her!" laughed Julie.

"And when she tripped our goalie and he fell backwards into the goal," roared Janie.

"How 'bout when she accidentally kicked the ball into her own goal?" Julie added.

The entire table of girls erupted with laughter. Alex laughed along with them. She had to. Janie was right. It had been funny.

Alex began to feel much better until she happened to glance at the next table. There sat Lorraine all by herself. She wasn't looking at Alex or her friends, but Alex was sure Lorraine had heard them.

"Shhhh," Alex warned her friends and nodded in Lorraine's direction.

After lunch, Alex and the other girls followed their classmates outside for recess. As Alex was going out the door, her teacher, Mr. Carpenter, called, "Alex, I forgot my whistle. Would you mind returning to the classroom and getting it for me? It is on my desk."

Alex hurried back inside and ran quickly to the classroom. Slowing her run at the door, she paused, then tiptoed to Mr. Carpenter's desk. Empty classrooms gave Alex the creeps. They were too silent, too unreal.

As Alex reached the desk, a sudden noise startled her. She stiffened and looked around. There it was again! Someone or something was in the coat closet.

Hardly breathing, Alex stood perfectly still and listened. What if it was a robber?

The noise sounded again. It was kind of like sniffling or crying. Was someone crying in the coat closet?

Alex tiptoed as quietly as she could in that direction and peeked around the partition that separated the classroom from the tiny room that held coats, schoolbags, and lunch boxes.

Lorraine! Alex almost gasped out loud. Lorraine sat all scrunched down in a corner of the closet. She was crying and clutching a tissue to her nose.

Alex backed quickly out of sight. Poor Lorraine. She was probably crying about the way everyone had laughed at her in the soccer game. Alex felt guilty. She had laughed, too.

Alex stood on the other side of the wall and tried to think of what to do. She could go in there and try to talk to Lorraine, but she didn't know what to say. She was sure Lorraine would be horribly embarrassed to know that Alex had seen her crying.

She could tell Mr. Carpenter that Lorraine was crying in the coat closet, but Alex wasn't sure that Lorraine would want her to do that, and anyway, that was almost like being a tattletale.

In the end, Alex did nothing. She tiptoed back to Mr. Carpenter's desk, grabbed the whistle, and left the room.

"Thank you, Alex," Mr. Carpenter responded as Alex gave him the whistle.

When Alex got home from school that afternoon, she told her mother about the soccer game and how she had discovered Lorraine crying in the coat closet.

"I really felt bad," Alex admitted. "I guess I felt sort of responsible because she was on my soccer team. You know, like maybe if I would have helped her she might not have played so badly and the kids wouldn't have laughed at her so much."

Mother put her arm around Alex's shoulders. "We don't always do the right thing because we are human and we are not perfect."

"Boy, you're not kidding," Alex agreed gloomily.

"But," Mother went on, "we have a perfect God who knows what to do and helps us correct our mistakes."

"How can I correct what happened today?" Alex wanted to know. "I mean, it already happened!"

"It is true that you cannot change what has happened," Mother said, "but can you do anything that might help Lorraine feel better?"

Alex thought for a moment. "Probably just being nice to Lorraine would help her. Not too many kids are nice to her."

"Why not?"

Alex spread her arms out wide. "I guess because she is fat," she explained.

"Oh, Alex, that's ridiculous," Mother exclaimed. "That's the same thing as being mean to people who are short or people who have brown hair!"

"I know," agreed Alex, "and some kids are extra mean. They call her 'Lardy Lorraine.' "

"Lardy Lorraine!" Mother cried. "That's terrible! A nickname like that could really hurt Lorraine."

"You mean by making her feel bad?" asked Alex.

"By making her feel bad about herself," Mother said. "If people keep calling her names, she might think that there really is something wrong with her. She may get so discouraged that she will quit trying to make friends. Or she will quit trying to do well in school or will quit trying to do anything. And that kind of attitude could affect the rest of her life," Mother added.

"Wow," Alex gasped. "I knew it was wrong to call people names, but I didn't know it would hurt them for the rest of their lives."

"It is a much bigger hurt than it seems," Mother said sadly. "That's why it is important to help children like Lorraine."

"But how do we help Lorraine?" Alex asked. "I guess we could say a prayer for her," she suggested.

"That's a good beginning," Mother smiled.

"What do you mean a good beginning?"

"Well, I don't know for sure," Mother admitted, "but it seems God might have more in mind for you to do to help Lorraine. After all, it seems almost as if He planned for you to find Lorraine crying in the coat closet."

"Like He planned for me to be the captain of Lorraine's soccer team," Alex added excitedly. She was beginning to have the feeling that God had, indeed, picked her to do something special for Lorraine.

"But what does God want me to do?" Alex asked her mother.

"I am sure God will show you," Mother answered. "Shall we say a prayer right now?"

"Okay," Alex bowed her head.

"Dear Father in Heaven," Mother prayed, "please help Lorraine to know that You love her and to feel good about herself. Please stop the children from making fun of her. And, please, dear God, show Alex what You want her to do to help Lorraine. Amen."

CHAPTER 2

Pyramid Smasher

"COME ON, JANIE, RUN!" Alex screamed at the top of her lungs. She had just finished running a mile around the school playground and was anxiously watching to see if her best friend would make her mile, too. If Janie didn't run her mile in ten minutes or less it wouldn't count, and Mr. Carpenter would not put a star by Janie's name on the chart.

"HURRY UP, JANIE," Alex screeched. She stole a peek at Mr. Carpenter's stopwatch. "YOU ONLY HAVE THIRTY SECONDS LEFT!"

Janie raced along the playground fence and circled the softball backstop. From there, she only had to run a short distance to where Alex and Mr. Carpenter were standing. Alex waved her arms, motioning for Janie to run her fastest.

Janie did. She threw her head back and gave it all that she could. Alex stared at her friend in surprise. She had never seen Janie run like that before.

As Janie passed in front of Mr. Carpenter, the teacher checked his watch. "Ten seconds to spare," he cried.

"HURRAH! YOU DID IT, JANIE!" Alex shouted.

Running over to Janie, Alex began clapping her on the back. "Congratulations! You now have four stars!"

Janie gasped for breath. "Alex," she panted, "do you have to be so embarrassing?"

"Huh?" Alex frowned and stared at her.

"Do you have to yell so loud?" Janie hissed. "Everybody is looking at me."

"So what?" Alex laughed. "You made your mile today. Aren't you happy?"

"Yeah," Janie admitted with a smile. "But I'm even happier that it is over with!"

Alex laughed again and put her arm across Janie's shoulders. Even though Janie didn't like to run or play sports as much as Alex did, she was still Alex's best friend.

Suddenly, Mr. Carpenter shouted, "Come on in, Lorraine!"

Alex jumped guiltily. She had forgotten all about Lorraine. Quickly, she stared across the playground at Lorraine. Why, she hadn't even made it past the swings—and she was walking not running!

"How is Lorraine ever going to make her mile if she doesn't run?" Alex frowned and put her hands on her hips.

"Maybe she can't," Janie replied.

"Can't what?" Alex asked.

"Maybe she can't run," Janie said.

"That's ridiculous, Janie! Everybody can run . . . can't they?"

Janie shrugged her shoulders. "Maybe she is too fat."

"She wasn't too fat to run when she was on the Tornadoes," Alex told Janie. The Tornadoes was the name of Alex's softball team.

Alex was the team's pitcher.

"Alex, that was two years ago. Lorraine hasn't been on the team since second grade," Janie reminded her.

"Really?" Alex asked, surprised. She was embarrassed to realize that she had not paid attention to Lorraine for two years.

The girls fell silent as Lorraine huffed and puffed her way to the blacktop. Alex inspected Lorraine carefully. She looked quite a bit bigger than she had in second grade. Alex began to wonder if Janie was right. Maybe Lorraine was too fat to run.

"HA, HA, HA! Look at this tree! It looks like it has a tummy ache!"

"Shut up, Joshua," yelled Alex. The trouble was that Joshua was right—her tree did look like it had a stomachache. She had wanted to draw a bent and crooked tree, but maybe she had drawn it a little too bent and crooked.

With a heavy sigh, Alex ripped the drawing off her pad of art paper and crumpled it into a ball. She waited until Joshua Barton turned his back and then threw it SMACK! at the back of his head.

"HEY!" Joshua yelled. He whirled around to see who had hit him.

The girls at Alex's table began to giggle. Joshua stared at them, then picked up the crumpled ball of paper and unfolded it. He frowned at Alex's drawing and carried it back to his table.

Uh oh, Alex thought, *now I have done it. He won't quit until he gets back at me.*

"Attention, class!" Mrs. Feather, the art teacher, clapped her hands. "Now that you have drawn your trees, we are going to take a look at trees that other artists have drawn."

Mrs. Feather stood several pictures of trees up on her desk. "This tree looks rather old, doesn't it?" she said, pointing to the first sketch. "See, it has a lot of branches that are all tangled together, and its trunk is rough and bumpy."

"Do you have any trees that look like they have stomachaches!" Joshua Barton asked Mrs. Feather.

Alex leaned forward in her chair and gave Joshua Barton her most ferocious stare.

"No," Mrs. Feather answered Joshua. The art teacher looked confused. "I don't think I have ever seen a picture of a tree that had a stomachache."

"Alex drew one!" Joshua cried gleefully. "Here it is." He held up the crumpled drawing for everyone to see.

Alex leaped from her seat and snatched the drawing out of Joshua's hand. Joshua laughed at Alex's angry face. Alex walked back to her table. She was shaking with anger. One more thing! Just let Joshua Barton do one more thing like that and she was going to clobber him!

Mrs. Feather frowned at Joshua and told him to sit down. She continued to talk about the tree sketches.

"I would think of this tree as fat," she told the class and pointed to a large, barrel-shaped evergreen.

"That must be Lardy Lorraine's tree!" whispered Joshua Barton. His whisper was loud enough for everyone in the class to hear.

Alex saw Lorraine's face turn red. Lorraine hunched down in her chair and covered her eyes. That was enough for Alex. Joshua Barton had gone too far today!

Without thinking what Mrs. Feather would say, Alex picked up a giant sponge that was lying on her table. It was wet and gooey from wiping up many spills. Taking aim, Alex flung the sponge at Joshua. BLAP! It hit the side of his face. Perfect shot!

"YEEAACK!" Joshua yelled. A muddy brown spot appeared on his face. Brown liquid dribbled down his neck.

Everyone in the class exploded into laughter. Everyone, that is, but Joshua, Mrs. Feather, and Alex. Mrs. Feather sent Joshua to the rest room to wash his face. Then she asked, "Who threw the sponge at Joshua?"

Alex stiffened. So did Janie beside her. The class became silent. Slowly, Alex raised her hand.

"Alex, I will see you out in the hall, please," ordered Mrs. Feather. Alex followed her

teacher outside the classroom door.

When they were alone in the hall, Mrs. Feather asked Alex, "Why did you throw a sponge at Joshua?"

"Oh, well, uh," Alex stammered, "I guess because it was the only thing I could find to throw at him."

A fleeting smile passed over the teacher's face. She shook her head and looked as sternly as she could at Alex. "That was not exactly the answer I was looking for. Why did you have to throw anything at Joshua?"

"Oh, I know it was wrong," Alex admitted. "And I am sorry, Mrs. Feather. It's just that Joshua Barton can be such a jerk!"

Mrs. Feather nodded her head in agreement. "Were you mad at him because he made fun of your tree?"

"Not really," Alex replied. "I was mad at him for making fun of Lorraine." And Alex began telling Mrs. Feather about how she had found Lorraine crying in the coat closet and how she wanted to help Lorraine.

When she had finished, Mrs. Feather smiled. "I am very impressed, Alex, that you care so much about Lorraine. We need more students like you."

"Even though I threw a sponge at Joshua?" Alex asked her teacher.

"Even so," Mrs. Feather replied. She put an arm around Alex's shoulders and they returned to the classroom.

"Come on, Alex, let's go!" Janie called. "My mom wants me home from school right away."

"Okay, wait a minute, Janie," Alex called back over her shoulder. She grabbed a younger boy's arm and said in his ear, "Jason, go get Rudy. We have to go now."

"But, Alex," Jason explained, "Rudy can't come right now. THE BULLDOZER is talking to him."

"What do you mean THE BULLDOZER is talking to him?" Alex frowned at Jason. Just the idea of having to talk to THE BULLDOZER after school made a shiver run up and down Alex's back. THE BULLDOZER had been Alex's second-grade teacher. She was now the teacher of Alex's seven-year-old brother, Rudy. Jason was Rudy's best friend and next-door neighbor.

"Why is THE BULLDOZER talking to Rudy?" Alex asked Jason again.

"Well," Jason replied, "you know that big tower of books in the library?"

"You mean the pyramid display?" Alex frowned. Of course she knew about the pyramid display. She and other fourth, fifth, and sixth graders had stayed after school every day for a whole week to help Mrs. Peoples, the librarian, stack 617 boxes into a cone-shaped pyramid. They had also decorated the boxes to look like books. The pyramid display was to be a major attraction at the first Kingswood Elementary open house of the year.

"What does the pyramid display have to do with Rudy?" Alex narrowed her eyes at Jason. She had a feeling that she was not going to like his answer.

"Well, uh, it wasn't exactly Rudy's fault," Jason began. "I mean, he didn't mean to make it fall down."

"WHAT?" Alex cried. She didn't wait to hear anymore but turned and raced to the library. Jason and Janie ran behind her.

"Brussels sprouts!" Alex groaned upon reaching the library door. The giant pyramid had collapsed in the middle of the room. Fallen book boxes lay scattered all across the library floor.

"Oh, no," Janie gasped as she and Jason caught up with Alex at the library door.

Alex put a finger to her lips and began

backing away. Mrs. Peoples might see her and might somehow think that it was Alex's fault for having such a troublesome brother as Rudy. Of course, Mrs. Peoples ought to know that Alex would not have picked out a brother like Rudy on purpose!

Alex, Janie, and Jason tiptoed around a corner and quickly made their way back down the hallway. They caught sight of Rudy slowly trudging his way up the same hallway.

"Goblin!" Alex shouted at her brother. "You are in trouble! And I mean trouble!" "Goblin" was Alex's special name for Rudy.

Rudy looked up at Alex miserably. "I didn't mean to. Honest, Alex. It just sorta happened."

Alex glared at her brother. "How does knocking over a whole pyramid just sort of happen?" she cried.

"Easy." Rudy started to explain. "See, I was checking out this book, *Air Raid on Jupiter,* but Steven Lupis kept trying to grab it out of my hands because he wanted it, too."

"Yeah?" Alex had heard about *Air Raid on*

Jupiter. It was a popular book among the second-grade boys.

"Well, anyway," Rudy continued, "I was running away from Steven and, well, not watching where I was going and I guess I sort of smashed into the pyramid."

"You should have seen it, Alex," Jason cried. "The whole thing crashed down on Rudy! It was awesome!"

"Awesome?" Rudy yelled at his best friend. "Oh, yeah, Jason. It was real awesome to be yelled at by THE BULLDOZER!" Rudy folded his arms across his chest and scowled down at the floor.

"It is not going to be too awesome when Mom and Dad find out about it, either," Alex reminded her brother.

"I have a note to give them from THE BULLDOZER," Rudy groaned. "Alex, do I have to give it to them?"

"Well," Alex said thoughtfully, "you could accidentally lose the note on the way home, or you could kind of forget to give it to Mom and Dad. But grown-ups have a way of finding out about things like that. And then you get in worse trouble."

"Yeah," Rudy agreed. "I better give them the note."

"Come on, Goblin," Alex sighed. "Let's get it over with."

CHAPTER 3

Miss Mushy

"Just think," Father commented as he dished a heaping spoonful of spaghetti onto Alex's plate, "I shall be known as the father of the famous pyramid smasher."

"Aw, Dad," Rudy groaned.

"Maybe the famous pyramid smasher will think about behaving himself if he spends some time by himself in his room," Mother remarked.

"But, Mom," Rudy protested, "it wasn't my fault!"

"Sure, Meatball, that's what they all say," put in Barbara, Rudy's oldest sister. Barbara was fourteen and in eighth grade. She would not let Alex and Rudy forget that not only was this her second year as a teenager, but also her second year in middle school.

"Well, it wasn't my fault," Rudy insisted. "Steven Lupis tried to grab a book out of my hand!"

"Rudy, lower your voice please. Barbara, do not call your brother Meatball. Alex, please pass me the salad dressing," Mother said.

"Sure, Mom," Alex passed the dressing to her mother and stuck her tongue out at her older sister.

"What was that for?" Barbara frowned at Alex.

Alex ignored the question and concentrated on trying to wrap the slippery strands of spaghetti around her fork. She was determined that they would not fall off. She stabbed her fork into a mass of noodles and twisted it slowly, keeping the fork pressed tightly against the bottom of the plate. The noodles began to turn with her fork. She slowly raised the fork to her mouth to take a bite but before she could WHOOSH! the noodles slipped off the fork.

Alex threw the fork down on her plate in frustration.

"*Ahem*," Father cleared his throat. "Rudy, do you really believe that what happened at the library was not your fault?"

"Well, if Steven Lupis hadn't tried to take my book away then nothing would have happened," Rudy replied, pushing out his lower lip.

"Let me see if I have this straight," Father said to Rudy. "You were standing around at the library, minding your own business, when, for no reason at all, Steven came up to you and tried to grab a book out of your hands."

"Right," replied Rudy.

"Hmmmmm." Father rubbed his chin. "You didn't make a face at him, or bump into him, or do anything like that?"

"Well, I did kind of push him," admitted Rudy. "But I didn't want him to get *Air Raid on Jupiter*."

"*Air Raid* on what?" Father asked.

"*Air Raid on Jupiter*, Dad," Alex answered. "It's one of those goofy second-grade books."

"It is not a goofy book!" Rudy hollered at Alex.

"All right, all right." Father held up his hands. "Do you think there might have been a better way to keep the book out of Steven's hands instead of pushing him?" he asked Rudy.

"I don't know . . . well . . . maybe," Rudy thought. "I guess I could have gone over to where Mrs. Peoples was standing."

Father nodded, "That might have prevented the pyramid crash."

"And kept me from getting into a lot of trouble," Rudy added. "But Steven Lupis started it!"

"I know, but you could have stopped it by simply walking away from him," Father pointed out. "You see, Rudy, it really doesn't matter who starts it. If you join a fight, you are just as wrong as the one who started it. As Christians, we are not supposed to join in on the fighting. We are supposed to try and stop it. That's called being peacemakers."

"But, Dad, sometimes it doesn't work to just walk away," Rudy said. "The bad kids will just follow you and try to keep fighting."

"Well, then you have to try something else," Father answered. "You can try saying something nice to whoever is starting the fight. Did you know that the Bible tells us that a soft word turns away anger?"

"Really?" Alex raised her eyebrows and looked at her father. "Do you mean that when Joshua Barton starts shooting off his big mouth at me that I should say, 'Why, Joshua, what a beautiful T-shirt you have on today?' "

Alex and Rudy collapsed into giggles. So did Mother and Barbara. Father roared his big, booming laugh.

"Brussels sprouts," Alex said, when everyone had calmed down. "It just might work. I mean, Joshua would be so surprised that he would probably shut up!"

"That reminds me," said Mother. "Are the children still calling Lorraine names?"

"Oh, sure," Alex answered. "That never stops. And I can't think of any way to help her."

"What are you two talking about?" Father asked.

Alex told Father about the soccer game and how she had found Lorraine crying in the coat closet.

"Sounds like Lorraine needs to start working out," Barbara commented after she had heard the story.

Alex stared at her sister. "You mean doing exercises and stuff?"

"Sure," Barbara answered, "or jogging."

"I don't think Lorraine can run," Alex told her sister.

"What?" exclaimed Barbara. "That's ridiculous. Everybody can run."

"I don't know," Alex replied. "Every time we run at school, all Lorraine does is walk."

"That's probably all she wants to do," Father chuckled. "I bet she could run a little way if she had to."

"Maybe." Alex looked doubtful.

"Look, Alex," Barbara explained, "what you should do when you are as fat as Lorraine is to start running a little bit. And each day, you run a little bit more. Pretty soon, you can run as far as you want. And at the same time, you are losing all that fat and slimming down."

"You mean it's that simple?" Alex cried in excitement. "All Lorraine has to do is to start running and her problems are over?"

Father, Mother, and Barbara laughed. Alex didn't join in the laughter. It sounded like a perfect solution to her. She would have to tell Lorraine about it tomorrow.

On the way to school the next morning, Alex told Janie about her plan for Lorraine.

"First we have to see how far Lorraine can run," Alex said excitedly.

"Alex . . ." Janie began.

"And then," Alex went on, too excited to notice Janie's frown, "she runs a little farther the next day."

"Alex . . ." persisted Janie.

"And then—" Alex tried to go on.

"Alex!" Janie cried loudly, stopping Alex in midsentence. "This is crazy!"

"Why?" Now it was Alex's turn to frown.

"Because Lorraine probably won't want to do it. Why should we spend our recesses trying

to make her do something she doesn't want to do?" replied Janie.

"What do you mean?" Alex asked. "Of course Lorraine will want to do it."

Janie sighed. "Don't you think she would have done it a long time ago if she'd wanted to? I mean, she has to know running is good for her. Our teachers tell us that all the time."

Alex fell silent. Could Janie be right? Would Lorraine not want to run? Alex shook her head. When she explained to Lorraine how great it would be to get in shape and not to be called fat anymore, Lorraine surely would be eager to start running. Why, anybody would!

"Good morning," Mr. Carpenter said to his class. "I have written tomorrow's math assignment on the blackboard. Copy it down quickly and we will move on to today's math homework."

Groans sounded throughout the room. Alex dug in her desk for a pencil and a piece of paper. How did her paper always get shoved to the very back of her desk? There were some not-too-wrinkled pieces under her spelling book. If only she could get her box of crayons out of the way and slide the paper out from under . . . WHAM! Alex's spelling book and box of crayons slammed to the floor.

Alex heard her classmates giggle and felt her teacher's eyes upon her. Red faced, she leaned over to pick up the book and crayons. Yanking a piece of paper out of her desk, she hurriedly copied down the math assignment from the blackboard.

Alex tried to concentrate on Mr. Carpenter's

math lesson. It was all full of integers and boring things. Her mind wanted to think about running and exercise instead. How was she going to talk Lorraine into running?

At last the bell rang for recess. Alex hurried outside. She quickly spotted Lorraine over by the swing set and hurried over to her. "Uh, hi, Lorraine," she stammered. Suddenly Alex lost her confidence. How was she going to tell Lorraine in a nice way that she was too fat and needed to run?

"Hi, Alex," Lorraine responded. She looked surprised to see Alex standing in front of her.

"Hi, Lorraine," Alex repeated. She shrugged her shoulders and dropped into the swing next to Lorraine. She busily dug a hole in the dirt with the toe of her shoe.

"Uh, Lorraine, I was wondering . . ." Alex began and then suddenly stopped at that moment because she became aware of a soccer ball whizzing out of nowhere and spinning right toward her!

Alex automatically reached up with her right foot and caught the ball on the top of her tennis shoe. She quickly pulled her foot back and on to the ground. The ball came to rest at her feet.

"Good trap, Alex," called Mr. Carpenter as he passed by the swing set on his walk around the playground.

"Yeah, good trap, Alex," someone echoed. It was Zack Logan. Alex liked Zack. He and his younger brother, Mark, lived one street over from Alex.

"Will you throw me the ball, Alex?" Zack called to her. He waved his arms at her.

Alex was tempted to keep the ball and make the boys mad. It was always fun to make them angry. The problem with that was they always had some way of getting back. Besides, she was going to concentrate on Lorraine today. She was just getting ready to throw the ball back to Zack when Joshua Barton ran over to her.

"Come on, Alex, quit fooling around. Give me the ball," he demanded.

Alex did not answer Joshua. In fact, she pretended that he wasn't even there. Very quickly, Alex threw the ball to Zack. Turning her back on Joshua, she began to swing.

Joshua angrily stomped back to the boys.

"Alex?" said a quiet voice.

"Did you say something?" Alex asked Lorraine.

"Yes," Lorraine answered shyly. "Would you show me how to do that?"

"Do what?" asked Alex, puzzled.

"How to trap a soccer ball," Lorraine replied.

"Oh, sure," Alex answered, surprised. She began to smile. Maybe this was a way to start Lorraine exercising.

"Come on," she told Lorraine, "let's go find a ball."

Alex and Lorraine looked all over the playground for a ball. The only one they could find that was not being used was an old basketball. It hardly bounced. It would not do at all.

Disgusted, Alex stared at Lorraine. "You know what we are going to have to do, don't you?" she asked her.

"No, what?" Lorraine questioned.

"We are going to have to steal the soccer ball from the boys!" Alex announced.

CHAPTER 4

Flattened Teacher

"Oh, Alex, how could we steal the ball from the boys?" Lorraine cried as she huffed and puffed along beside Alex.

"I've got a plan," Alex said in a hushed voice. She looked around to make sure no one else was listening.

"I'll stand on that side." Alex pointed to the far side of the soccer field. "You stand on this side. When I see a good chance to get the ball, I'll rush onto the field and kick it over to you. You run with it to the blacktop where Mr. Carpenter is standing."

"But what if you can't get it away from the boys?" Lorraine asked.

"Don't worry. I'll get it away from them," Alex answered confidently.

"But what if . . ."

"Quit worrying," Alex interrupted. "Just run your fastest to the blacktop." A moment later she stopped in her tracks. "You *can* run, can't you?" she asked Lorraine.

"Of course I can run," Lorraine answered.

Alex left Lorraine and trotted behind the goal and around the soccer field to its far side.

Joshua Barton saw her. "No girls allowed!!" he hollered.

"Aw, cut it out, Josh," cried Zack. "It's only Alex."

"Yeah, and we need more players," called Aaron, one of the goalies. "Come on, Alex, be on our team!"

Alex stuck her tongue out at Joshua and took her place on the front line. This was even better than she had planned. She should have no trouble getting the ball now.

Before the kickoff, Alex quickly looked in Lorraine's direction. Lorraine signaled that she was ready.

Zack kicked off, passing the ball to Adam, another forward. Adam passed it back to Zack, who, in trying to get the ball around Joshua, shot it over to Alex. Alex dribbled it down the right side of the field, close to the line.

"SHOOT IT, ALEX, SHOOT IT!" Zack screamed. Alex hesitated. She would love to shoot a goal, especially against Joshua Barton's team. But out of the corner of her eye, she could see Lorraine standing to her right, not six feet away. If she didn't get it to Lorraine now, she might not have another chance.

"SORRY, ZACK!" she hollered and kicked the ball off the field in a straight line to Lorraine.

"What are you doing, Alex?" Zack shouted.

"Hey, Alex, the goal's the other way!" Joshua pointed.

The ball reached Lorraine and, somehow, she caught it.

"RUN, LORRAINE, RUN!" Alex yelled.

"What's going on?" the boys cried.

Lorraine began a slow dash toward the blacktop.

"Hey!" the boys cried again. "Come back here with our ball!"

The boys chased after Lorraine. So did Alex. They all charged for the blacktop and Mr. Carpenter.

Suddenly, Lorraine tripped and rolled on the ground. The ball shot out of her hands. Two boys fell over her. Alex recovered the ball before the boys could reach it and dribbled it furiously to the blacktop. Joshua, Zack, and the others followed, hot on her trail.

"Alex! Wait!" Mr. Carpenter shouted and waved his arms at her. "Alex! Stop!" But it was too late. Alex couldn't stop. She and the ball and Joshua Barton and Zachary Logan crashed into Mr. Carpenter, knocking their teacher to the ground. The children fell on top of him.

BAM! WHAM! OOOOOH! OW! Shrieks and moans erupted from the pile of arms and legs.

Mr. Carpenter struggled to sit up. He did not say a word but just stared at Alex. Then, Mr. Carpenter gave Alex a smile—not an ordinary pleasant smile—but a "you are in trouble" smile.

"Alexandria Brackenbury, would you mind explaining why we are all lying in a heap on the blacktop?" Mr. Carpenter asked.

The boys snickered. They were not the least bit sorry to see Alex get in trouble. After all, she had stolen their soccer ball and ruined their game.

Alex swallowed hard and began to explain. "Well, uh, I was gonna teach Lorraine how to trap a soccer ball."

At this, the boys hooted with laughter.

Mr. Carpenter held up his hands for them to be quiet. "Yes, go on, Alex," he ordered.

"Uh, and there was no other soccer ball to use so . . ."

"So you decided to steal our ball!" Joshua accused.

"Quiet!" Mr. Carpenter responded. "Any more interruptions and you will miss your next recess. Go on, Alex."

Alex twisted the buttons on her jacket nervously. "I guess we did sort of steal their ball, but that was because it's the only soccer ball around here. We were gonna bring it to you and ask you if we could have a turn to use it," Alex finished weakly. She looked away from her teacher's frowning face. Her plan of getting the ball away from the boys did not sound like such a good idea now.

Mr. Carpenter said nothing in reply. The school bell rang signaling the end of recess. Mr. Carpenter cleared his throat. "I believe we will discuss this matter during the next recess."

Alex gulped. It sounded like she and Lorraine were in big trouble.

That afternoon when the bell rang for recess, Alex and Lorraine remained seated at their desks. The other children went outside.

Mr. Carpenter leaned both hands on a desk and gazed thoughtfully at Alex and Lorraine. Alex could hardly look at her teacher. She glanced up at him and back down at her desk. No one spoke for several seconds.

Then Mr. Carpenter broke the silence. "Don't you think it would have been a better idea for you to have come to me first and explain your situation rather than to steal the ball from the boys?"

Alex and Lorraine nodded their heads.

"I'll tell you what," Mr. Carpenter suggested. "To be fair, I will let the boys use the soccer ball in the morning recess and the girls can use it in the afternoon recess."

"Okay," Alex and Lorraine quickly responded.

"If you want to play with a ball and it's not your turn, then you can play with a red ball." Mr. Carpenter was referring to a supply of red balls that were kept in the gym.

Alex made a face. "Those red balls are always out of air," she complained.

Mr. Carpenter paused and smiled at Alex. This time it was a "you asked for it" smile. "The balls won't be out of air after you and Lorraine get through with them," he said.

"What do you mean?" Alex asked.

Mr. Carpenter motioned for her and Lorraine to follow him. He had a "you will find out" smile on his face.

Alex and Lorraine followed their teacher down the hall and into the gym. Ms. Springate looked surprised to see them.

"Good afternoon, Ms. Springate," said Mr. Carpenter. "These two young ladies believe that our supply of red balls could use a little air. Is your pump available?"

"Why, yes, Mr. Carpenter," Ms. Springate answered, looking even more surprised. "But I don't have time right now to pump up all the red balls."

"I was not asking you to pump the balls," Mr. Carpenter explained. "I am sure Alex and Lorraine would love to do the job."

Alex and Lorraine helped Mr. Carpenter pull a number of red balls out of a giant wire container and drop them on the gymnasium floor. Alex counted the balls. Eleven! She and Lorraine had to pump up eleven balls.

Mr. Carpenter showed the girls how to use the pump. "Pump hard," he told them before he left. "You will stay in as many recesses as it takes to pump up all the red balls."

Alex and Lorraine frowned at one another. Glancing at the clock on the gymnasium wall told Alex that there were only ten minutes of recess left.

"Brussels sprouts!" Alex exclaimed. "Do you think we can pump up eleven balls in ten minutes?"

Lorraine looked doubtful. "We can try," she replied.

The girls felt awkward using the pump. They did their best and worked as fast as they could, but by the time the bell rang, they had pumped only three balls.

As they shuffled back to the classroom, Alex tried to figure how many more recesses they would need to finish pumping up all of the balls.

"If we pumped three balls in ten minutes this recess, that means we can do six balls next recess because then we'll have twenty minutes," she told Lorraine.

"Right," Lorraine agreed, "and then we'll only have two more left."

"Yeah, and we will have to stay in another recess to finish them," sighed Alex gloomily. "I'm sorry, Lorraine, I guess I really got us in trouble."

"Oh, that's okay," Lorraine responded

cheerfully. "At least now I have something to do at recess."

Alex glanced sharply at Lorraine. What did she mean she would have something to do at recess? Did she usually have nothing to do at recess? How awful!

That evening at dinner, Barbara asked Alex, "Did you start Lorraine on her exercise program today?"

Alex stabbed at the peas on her plate and sighed. It was just like Miss Mushy to bring up an unpleasant subject. Alex tried to ignore her sister.

"Alex," Mother said, "your sister asked you a question."

Alex sighed again. She gave up trying to stab a particular pea with her fork. She looked around at her family wondering how she was going to tell them about knocking Mr. Carpenter to the ground.

"We are all holding our breath for your answer," teased Father.

Alex took a big breath and said in a rush, "I

stole the soccer ball from the boys. They chased me and Lorraine. I ran into Mr. Carpenter and knocked him down on the blacktop. Lorraine and I got in trouble and we have to blow up eleven balls at recess!"

No one else spoke for several seconds. Finally, Father said, "I am almost sorry I asked."

Mother, looking surprised, said, "Alex, would you mind explaining all of that a little more clearly?"

Alex told her family how she and Lorraine had stolen the soccer ball from the boys and how she had run into Mr. Carpenter on the blacktop.

"He wasn't hurt, was he?" Mother asked worriedly.

"No," Alex answered, "but, boy, was he mad!"

After dinner, Alex curled up beside her puppy, T-Bone, on the living room carpet. T-Bone did not look much like a puppy anymore. He would be one year old at Christmastime and was already a full-grown Labrador.

Father entered the living room and sat down

in his favorite chair. Alex raised her head and quickly scanned the area. No one else was around. Darting across the room, Alex leaped into her father's lap.

"Whoa, Firecracker!" Father laughed. "You mean, I rate above the dog?" he teased.

Alex ignored that question and laid her head back on his shoulder.

"Sounds like you had a tough day," Father said.

Alex nodded. They sat silent for a while.

Finally, Alex broke the silence. "Lorraine said something really strange today," she told her father.

"What was that, Firecracker?"

"Well, it sounded like she was glad that we have to stay in at recess and pump up balls. She said that at least she would have something to do at recess."

"Really?" Father frowned. "What does Lorraine usually do at recess? Does she have any special friends she plays with?"

"That's just it," Alex replied. "I don't think Lorraine has any friends at school."

"Hmmmm." Father rubbed his chin. "Sounds like Lorraine needs you to champion her."

"Huh?" Alex asked. "What do you mean 'champion her'?"

"To champion somebody means to encourage and help that person and to stick up for him or her."

"Really?" Alex was surprised. "I thought a champion was somebody who was the best at doing something."

"That's right, too," Father agreed. "Champion means both of those things. And sometimes it takes a champion to be able to champion another person. Do you understand what I mean?"

"I think so," Alex said slowly. "You mean it takes someone really strong to be able to stand up for someone else."

"Right," said Father. He looked deep into Alex's eyes. "You are that kind of champion, Alex."

CHAPTER 5

Explosion in the Gym

The next morning at recess, Alex and Lorraine walked down the hall to the gym instead of going outside with their classmates.

"Hey, Brackenbury!" Joshua Barton hollered after Alex, "Have fun pumping!"

"Yeah," the other boys laughed. "Make sure you get those balls full of air!"

The boys pushed their arms up and down as if operating imaginary pumps. They "pumped" all the way out the door.

Alex rolled her eyes toward the ceiling. Those boys were impossibly ridiculous. Lorraine giggled.

The girls set to work immediately upon reaching the gym. Before they knew it, they had pumped up seven balls. Those seven plus the three they had pumped the day before made ten out of the eleven balls that needed pumping.

"One more ball to go!" Lorraine and Alex shouted.

"Hurry up," Alex told Lorraine as she steadied the last ball on the gym floor. "We don't want to be stuck inside another recess for one stupid ball."

"I'm pumping as hard as I can," Lorraine panted after a few seconds of hard work. "This ball just won't pump up."

"Here, let me try," Alex demanded. She grabbed the pump and worked her arms up and down furiously.

"Whew!" she gasped after a while. "What's the matter with this ball?"

"Maybe it has a hole in it," Lorraine suggested. "It's really old. See, it's more pink than red."

Suddenly, the bell ending recess rang. Mr. Carpenter came to the door of the gym but neither girl saw him. They were too intent on watching the ball.

Mr. Carpenter called, "Girls, it's time to stop. . . ."

At that moment, Alex gave an extra hard push on the pump. WHAM! The ball exploded and fell apart in Lorraine's hands.

Lorraine screamed and dropped the ball. Alex stared in amazement. The ball lay on the floor in two pieces.

Mr. Carpenter strode quickly across the gym to the girls. "Anyone hurt?" he asked. Alex and Lorraine shook their heads. The teacher picked up the pieces of what used to be a ball.

"When I asked you to blow up the red balls, I didn't mean for you to actually blow them up!" Mr. Carpenter chuckled.

"I'm sorry," Alex replied. "I didn't mean to blow it up. I mean, I didn't mean to blow it apart!"

"I know you didn't," Mr. Carpenter smiled. "Ordinarily, I don't think you could explode a ball. There must have been something wrong with this one. It looks pretty old for one thing. Don't worry about it," he assured them. "I'll tell Ms. Springate about it. Go on back to class."

Alex and Lorraine started across the gym to the door. "Oh, Alex," Mr. Carpenter called after them, "the next time I have a flat tire, I'll be sure to call on you to pump it up."

It didn't take long for the story to spread through the classroom. By the time Mr. Carpenter returned, the entire class knew about the exploded ball.

"Hey, Tarzan!" a boy teased Alex. "Did you get all those muscles from swinging through the trees?"

"Naw, she's really King Kong and got them from climbing buildings!" cried another boy.

Alex gritted her teeth. One of these days she was going to clobber a few of those boys.

At afternoon recess, Mr. Carpenter let Alex and Lorraine play with the soccer ball. Alex made a face at the boys as she and Lorraine passed them.

On their way to the field, Alex and Lorraine stopped at the swings. There Janie and several other girls were busy spinning themselves around and around on the swings.

"Janie," Alex called. "Do you want to come to the soccer field with us?" She held the ball up triumphantly.

"No, thank you," Janie replied curtly.

"Aw, Janie, come on," Alex pleaded. "We have the soccer ball."

"I'd rather swing," Janie told her. "Why don't you stay and swing with me?"

Alex stared at Janie in confusion. Had Janie forgotten her plans for Lorraine to begin running at recess? How could she remind her with Lorraine standing so close by?

"Well, uh, Lorraine and I thought we would kind of work out with the soccer ball," Alex said to Janie. She said the words *work out* in a loud voice and hoped that Janie would understand her meaning.

"Okay," Janie shrugged, "have fun."

Alex frowned. There was nothing else for her to do but go on to the soccer field without Janie. As she reached the edge of the field, Alex felt Lorraine suddenly tap her shoulder.

"Did you know we are being followed?" Lorraine asked.

Alex turned around. "Brussels sprouts!" she gasped. A line of boys was marching behind her and Lorraine.

"Come on," she said in a low voice. "Just ignore them and maybe they'll go away."

Alex led Lorraine to the center of the field. The boys sat down around the edge of the field and watched them.

"Uh, Alex," Lorraine whispered. "I don't think they are going to leave."

Alex put her hands on her hips. "ALL RIGHT, YOU GUYS, WHAT ARE YOU

DOING HERE?" she hollered at the boys.

"WE CAN GO ANYWHERE WE WANT TO AT RECESS!" one of them hollered back.

"YEAH! IT'S A FREE COUNTRY!" shouted another.

"WON'T YOU TEACH US HOW TO PLAY SOCCER, ALEX?" called a smart-aleck voice. It was Joshua Barton's.

The other boys laughed.

Alex looked around the playground for Mr. Carpenter. At last she spotted him. He was standing a few yards away. It looked like he was watching them. He had a smile on his face!

"Okay, if that's the way he wants it," Alex snapped angrily.

"Who?" Lorraine asked.

"Never mind," Alex hissed. "Just throw me the ball."

"Huh?"

"You want to learn how to trap, right? Then throw me the ball high—real high."

Lorraine backed away from Alex and positioned herself to throw the ball. Alex nervously got ready for the throw. It would not do to miss the ball with all the boys and Mr. Carpenter watching her.

Lorraine must have also felt nervous because instead of throwing the ball toward Alex, she heaved it straight up in the air over her head. Alex knew she did not have much chance to trap that ball so she decided to head the ball back to Lorraine instead. At least that would look better than missing it completely.

Getting under the ball as it fell back toward the ground, Alex leaped high in the air and met it with her head. Unfortunately, she hit it with the top of her head instead of with her forehead. The ball bounced high in the opposite direction. It soared over the fence and into the creek that ran behind the school.

The boys rolled on the ground, holding their stomachs and laughing uproariously. Mr. Carpenter walked over to Alex and Lorraine. "Alex, I don't know how you do these things," he said, shaking his head.

"Me, neither," Alex sighed.

"How good are you at climbing fences?" he asked.

"Excellent," replied Alex.

"Then go get the ball out of the creek, please," Mr. Carpenter ordered. "But, Alex," he called after her, "please take it easy on the fence—don't knock it down or explode it or anything."

"Very funny, very funny," Alex grumbled as she vaulted over the top of the fence. How was she ever going to live this one down? The boys would never stop teasing her.

Alex retrieved the ball and climbed back over the fence. She leaned against the fence and did not move. She was not going back to where the boys were for anything.

Mr. Carpenter seemed to understand. He chased the boys away from the soccer field.

Alex returned to the field and sat down beside Lorraine. She stretched her legs out in front of her and leaned back on her elbows. Why had everything gone wrong? So far, all of her attempts to help Lorraine had not worked. In fact, she hadn't even been able to tell Lorraine about her running idea.

Alex sat straight up. She could tell her now!

This was a perfect time to talk to Lorraine. But what if Janie was right? What if Lorraine didn't want to do it? She glanced at Lorraine sitting so quietly beside her. Well, she would have to tell her sooner or later. It might as well be now.

Taking a big breath, Alex asked, "Lorraine, how would you like to start running?"

"Huh?" Lorraine stared at Alex with wide open eyes.

"How would you like to start running?" Alex repeated. "I would do it with you. Every day we could run a little bit farther than the day before until you get in shape."

Lorraine continued to stare at Alex as if she couldn't believe what Alex was saying. Alex talked faster and faster, trying to convince Lorraine of her idea.

"Pretty soon you would be running a whole mile every day and you wouldn't be fat and the kids wouldn't call you names anymore."

Still there was no answer from Lorraine. The same surprised look remained on her face.

"What do you say?" Alex finally asked.

Lorraine cleared her throat. She started to say something, but instead, she burst into tears.

Alex was shocked. "Oh, Lorraine, I'm sorry," she apologized. "I didn't mean to hurt your feelings, honest!"

"Oh, no, it's not that," Lorraine sniffed. "It's just that nobody ever bothered to help me get in shape before, and, well, it's really neat, and, oh, I'm sorry I'm being such a crybaby!"

"Oh, that's okay," replied Alex. Then she laughed as Lorraine blew her nose on a leaf.

"You know, Lorraine," Alex said thoughtfully. "I don't think it means that the kids at school don't want to help you. They just don't think about it. They don't notice how bad it is for you."

"But you noticed," Lorraine pointed out.

"That's different," Alex declared. "God helped me to notice."

"Really? He did?" Lorraine looked surprised. "How?"

"Oh, lots of ways," answered Alex. She told Lorraine how she had seen her crying in the coat closet and how she had felt that God had wanted her to help Lorraine.

"Wow!" breathed Lorraine. "I didn't even think God would want to help me."

The bell rang to end recess. Alex and Lorraine walked back up to the blacktop.

"Alex," Lorraine said timidly, "there's still one thing I would like to do."

"What's that?" Alex asked.

"Learn how to trap a soccer ball," Lorraine replied.

Alex laughed and led the way inside.

CHAPTER 6

Spies

"I still don't see why you have to spend so much time with Lorraine," Janie complained to Alex. "You're with her every recess!"

"That's because we practice running in the morning and soccer in the afternoon," Alex tried to explain.

"But when are you going to play with me?" Janie frowned. "Is Lorraine more important to you than me?"

"No, of course not," Alex answered. "You are my *best* friend. But Lorraine really needs my help. My mom says that sometimes when kids get made fun of by other kids, it hurts them for their whole lives. I'm trying to help Lorraine so that kids will stop calling her names, and anyway, I think God wants me to."

"Oh, Alex," Janie cried, "sometimes I wish you weren't always such a good Christian!"

"Janie!" Alex covered her mouth with both hands. "How could you say such a thing?"

"I don't know," Janie moaned and collapsed in the nearest chair. "I'm sorry."

Alex stared for a while at her best friend. Then she sighed. "Come on, Janie. Let's forget about Lorraine and have fun spending the night together. What movie do you want to watch?"

"I don't care," Janie replied. "What do you want to watch?"

"Well, how about *An American Tail*?" Alex suggested. "We haven't seen that for awhile."

"Okay," agreed Janie. "Tony and Bridget are so cute the way they fall in love with each other. Don't you think so?"

"Oh, sure, Janie," Alex said to keep her friend happy. She wrinkled her nose in disgust. Why did Janie always like the mushy stuff?

"Hey, Dad, we are ready!" Alex called.

Father turned on the VCR and stared at the supply of potato chips, candy bars, and cherry cola balanced in the middle of the sofa. "Are you sure you haven't forgotten anything?" he asked. "Perhaps you would like to add a bowl of popcorn?"

"We'll get that later," Alex assured him.

It wasn't too long after that—about the time Fievel Mousekewitz boarded the ship to America—that four teenagers tromped through the family room and in front of the television set on their way to the basement.

Alex and Janie looked up in surprise. It was Barbara and her best friend, Heather. And following them were two boys!

Janie and Alex stared at one another. "Are those their boyfriends?" Janie asked excitedly.

"How should I know?" Alex replied, annoyed. Leave it to Miss Mushy to barge in here and interrupt the movie. Now Janie might be more interested in the teenagers downstairs than in the movie.

Sure enough, a minute later Janie whispered to Alex, "Do you want to sneak downstairs and spy on them?"

Alex pretended that she hadn't heard Janie.

"Alex!" Janie shouted. "I know you heard me."

Alex sighed. "Janie, don't you want to watch the movie?"

"Oh, sure," Janie answered. "After we sneak downstairs."

Alex groaned.

"Oh, come on, Alex, just one time?" Janie pleaded. "I don't have an older sister like you so I don't get to see what teenagers are like."

"You are lucky," Alex retorted.

"Can't we go down just once?" Janie insisted. "Call your dad and ask him to stop the movie."

"Okay, okay," Alex grumbled.

After Father left the room, Alex and Janie crept down the basement stairs, one at a time. When they reached the bottom, they carefully opened the basement door, just a crack.

Loud music blasted their ears. Janie quickly stepped behind Alex. She motioned for Alex to peek around the door. Alex made a face. She always had to do the hard part. Janie was either too scared or too embarrassed.

Alex took a deep breath and stuck her head around the door. "They are on the other side of the play area, you know—where the stereo is," she whispered.

Janie nodded.

"I don't think they would see us if we crawled into the room," Alex suggested. She was beginning to like this adventure. "We could hide inside Rudy's play teepee."

The girls giggled with excitement and dropped to their hands and knees. They crawled rapidly across the floor to a small plastic tent. The teepee rocked alarmingly as both girls dove inside it.

"*Shhhhh,*" Alex hissed to keep herself as well as Janie from breaking into loud giggles. They sat covering their mouths with their hands for what seemed like hours. The music continued to rock. No one came to yank them out of the teepee. "I think we're safe," Alex whispered.

"Now what do we do?" Janie wanted to know.

"How should I know?" Alex replied. "It

was your idea to spy on them."

"Okay, okay, so let's be spies," Janie decided. She bravely poked her head out of the teepee.

"Oh, Alex, look, they're dancing!"

Alex rolled her eyes upward. "I told you teenagers are boring."

"It's fun to watch them," replied Janie.

"Oh, okay.," Alex peeked out of the teepee with Janie. Actually, sometimes she did like to watch Miss Mushy and her friends. She remembered last summer when her sister had a friend over who did back flips to music. Now, that had been really awesome.

Suddenly, the music stopped.

"Hey, let's play Ping-Pong!" one of the boys suggested.

"Uh oh," Alex whispered to Janie. The teepee sat right beside the Ping-Pong table. Alex quickly adjusted the door flap so that it covered the teepee door as much as possible.

Suddenly Father's voice boomed down the stairs, "Anybody seen Alex?" Alex and Janie exchanged frightened glances.

"No," Barbara answered her father.

"That's funny. I can't find them anywhere," said Father, whose voice sounded to Alex as if he was coming down the stairs. Alex and Janie sat as if glued to the floor. They didn't move a muscle.

"Have you tried Alex's room?" Barbara asked.

"Well, I called up the stairs, but I didn't actually go up there," Father admitted. His voice sounded to Alex like it was getting closer and closer. Alex could see out of a tiny crack in the teepee's flap. Her heart skipped a beat when Father's shoes suddenly moved into sight! *He is standing right in front of the teepee,* Alex told herself.

"Well, maybe I'll go up to Alex's room," Father said. His shoes moved out of sight. Alex took a breath and wiped imaginary sweat off her forehead. That had been a close call. But now what were they going to do? They couldn't move out of the teepee until Barbara and her friends quit playing Ping-Pong.

WHAP! Something hard bounced off the

side of the teepee. It had barely missed hitting Janie's head.

"Hey, Heather," Alex heard a boy tease. "Try keeping the ball on the table." Footsteps ran past the teepee as someone ran after the Ping-Pong ball.

Alex and Janie gave each other frightened looks. They ducked their heads to the floor and hoped no more balls would hit the teepee. The game above their heads sounded fast and furious—the ball slapped against each end of the table in double time.

Suddenly, the thing that Alex worried about most happened. The ball bounced off the table, rolled across the floor, and underneath the flap of the teepee! Alex, not knowing what else to do, rolled the ball back underneath the flap to the outside.

"Hey! Did you see that?" cried one of the boys.

"Come on, Brett, get the ball," called his friends.

"No, wait a minute," Brett said. "This is weird. The ball rolled into this tent thing. And then it rolled right back out again!"

"So?" asked the other boy.

"So, it couldn't roll back out unless somebody threw it out," Brett insisted.

"Well, maybe it's haunted," the other boy teased.

"Aha!" cried Barbara. "I think I know who the ghosts are!" She stomped over to the teepee and threw open the flap. "ALEXANDRIA BRACKENBURY! YOU COME OUT OF THERE!"

Alex slowly raised her head and smiled sheepishly at her sister. Janie scrunched down low behind Alex.

"DAD! DAD!" Barbara's voice bellowed up the stairs. Alex could hear her father's footsteps racing down the stairs.

"Good heavens," she heard him answer. "What now? A fire? A flood? Maybe an avalanche?"

"Two ghosts," Barbara replied. "Look!"

Father's face suddenly stared at Alex through the teepee flap. "*Hmmmm.*" He stroked his chin and rocked back on his heels.

"Two rather puny looking ghosts if I do say so myself."

"Get them out of there, Dad!" Barbara fumed.

Father cleared his throat. "Uh, ghosties," he sang in a low voice, "I think you should come out now."

Alex looked her father in the eye. "Do we have to, Dad?" she whispered.

Father raised his eyebrows in surprise. "What do you want to do? Spend the night in the teepee?"

Alex and Janie nodded their heads vigorously. They were too embarrassed to come out and face the teenagers.

"Alex, if you don't get out of there, we are going to drag you out," warned Barbara.

Alex quickly whispered one word to Janie, "RUN!" The girls dashed across the room and up the stairs before anyone else could say a word. They did not stop running until they were safely behind the door to Alex's bedroom.

"Whew!" Alex sighed and collapsed on her bed.

"How embarrassing!" Janie moaned and flopped down beside Alex.

"May I come in?" Father called from the hallway.

"Yes," Alex answered. The smiles vanished from their faces. They sat up straight on the bed. Were they in trouble?

Father opened the door. "A very cute young man is waiting for you downstairs in the family room," he told Alex and Janie with a wink.

"Who?" both girls gasped. Surely not one of Miss Mushy's friends.

"Fievel Mousekewitz," Father replied. He laughed at the relief on their faces. "Come on," he urged them. "Your mother just took pizza and milk shakes down to the group in the basement. That ought to hold them for a while. I think it's safe for you to finish watching your movie."

"Pizza and milk shakes!" Alex cried. "Do we get any?"

"Ho, ho!" Father boomed. "And what about all those treats I saw piled on the sofa?"

"Oh, that," replied Alex. "We ate those a long time ago, didn't we, Janie?"

"Right," Janie agreed.

"Come on, you two," Father held the door open. "Show time begins in one minute! Pizza and shakes will be served."

"YIPPEE!" cried Alex and Janie. They skipped out of the room and down the stairs to keep their date with Fievel Mousekewitz.

CHAPTER 7

The Bulldozer

"Good dribbling! Come on, Lorraine, keep going . . . keep going. All right! Way to go!" Alex clapped her hands.

Lorraine collapsed to the ground, swallowing big gulps of air. She had just succeeded in dribbling the soccer ball around the entire soccer field.

"I knew you could do it, Lorraine!" Alex told her. "Now rest a minute while I set up these rocks."

Walking to the middle of the field, Alex plopped down a large, roundish rock. After taking several steps backward, she plopped down another one. Alex repeated this procedure until she had placed five rocks on the ground, several feet apart from each other.

"Okay, Lorraine," she called, "let's practice dribbling around these rocks."

Alex and Lorraine each dribbled up and down the field several times, being sure to circle each rock. Alex watched Lorraine carefully. She was definitely getting better. She didn't lose control of the ball as much and she could dribble at a slow jogging speed. Lorraine's running was a lot better, too. Now she could run all the way around the playground once—at a very slow speed, of course.

"Well," Alex told herself, "it's only been a week since we first started working out. Give Lorraine another week and she'll probably make her mile!"

The bell to end recess rang and the two girls started for the blacktop.

"What about the rocks?" Lorraine asked.

"Leave 'em there," Alex waved her hand. "We will use them tomorrow."

At the edge of the blacktop, the girls met the boys, who were coming from the softball field.

"Hey, coach," Joshua Barton yelled at Alex. "How's it going?"

Alex scowled at Joshua.

"Aw, don't pay attention to him," Zack told Alex. He and Aaron walked beside Alex and Lorraine.

"How is it going?" Aaron asked Alex.

"Pretty good, really," Alex answered. "Lorraine's getting better at dribbling and she can run pretty far now."

"Yeah, we noticed that this morning," said Zack.

"See, Lorraine?" Alex shook Lorraine's shoulder. "It's not just me. Other people think you are doing good, too."

Lorraine's face beamed with happiness at the praise.

"Hey, you know what we ought to do?" Aaron lowered his voice and looked at the others with excitement. "We ought to make up a soccer play with Lorraine in it and use it in gym. That would blow Joshua's mind!"

Alex slapped her knee with her hand. "Great idea! But when can we figure out the play?"

"How about after school at your house?" Zack asked Alex.

"Fine with me," Alex shrugged.

"Excuse me," a deep voice suddenly sounded.

The children looked around. Mr. Carpenter stood over them, his arms folded across his chest, his foot tapping against the blacktop.

"Whenever you are ready," he told them, "we can all go inside."

Giggling nervously, the four children hurried inside.

After school, Alex, Lorraine, Janie, Aaron, and Zack stood on the front steps of the school building. They were waiting for Rudy and Jason.

"Where could they be?" Alex frowned.

"Who knows," Janie sighed. "Maybe they're flying paper airplanes in the bathroom again!"

"No, I don't think so," Alex chuckled. "Rudy got in too much trouble for that."

"Rudy sounds like quite a character," Aaron said.

"Oh, he is," Zack told him. "Rudy's the one

who single-handedly knocked down the pyramid in the library."

"Really?" Aaron looked impressed.

"Here he is!" Janie suddenly announced.

They all turned to look as Rudy, leaning heavily on Jason, hobbled through the door and walked stiff legged down the steps.

"What happened to you, Goblin?" Alex exclaimed.

Rudy frowned and stuck out his lower lip. "I busted my knee, see?" He raised his pant leg to show Alex his injury. A square gauze bandage was taped across his right knee.

"How'd you do that?" she asked.

"Tripped over a rock playing soccer," Rudy grumbled. "There were a bunch of rocks in the field."

"Rocks on the soccer field?" Alex repeated. She and Lorraine exchanged guilty looks. "Were they, uh, big rocks, all lined up in a row, with enough space to dribble around them?"

"Yeah," Rudy answered, "how did you know?"

Alex sighed deeply. "Because I put them there. Lorraine and I were dribbling around them at recess. I didn't think about anybody else playing on the field."

Rudy scowled at her. "My own sister!"

"I'm sorry, Goblin," Alex replied. "I didn't mean for you to get hurt. I just didn't think about moving the rocks off the field."

"Well, you better get them off pretty quick," Rudy told her. "THE BULLDOZER is supermad about it!"

"She is?" Alex's voice cracked. "What did she say?"

"That if she finds out who put those rocks in the field, she is going to make sure that they get punished!"

"She said that?" Alex sank to the ground and buried her face in her hands.

"Alex, don't worry. We'll think of something." Janie tried to make her friend feel a little better.

"Yeah, THE BULLDOZER doesn't know it was you," said Aaron. "And none of us will tell her."

"She'll find out," Alex moaned. "Teachers always find out."

"Not always," Zack said. "Come on. Let's go get the rocks off the field. Maybe that will help to calm down THE BULLDOZER."

The children ran behind the school building to the soccer field. The older children picked up the rocks and began to carry them off the field. A loud blast from a whistle stopped them short. Alex knew without turning around who had blown that whistle.

An enormous figure in tall, black boots hurriedly strode across the playground. Her arms swung at her sides in perfect rhythm with her steps. One, two, one, two. . . .

"Where do you think you are going with those rocks?" THE BULLDOZER hollered. She looked directly at Alex.

"Brussels sprouts," Alex whispered to the others. "I'm done for."

"Alexandria Brackenbury, I asked you a question," the teacher snapped. "What are you doing with those rocks?"

"Oh, uh, well, uh," Alex stammered and

shifted her weight from one leg to the other. "We are getting them off the field so nobody else gets hurt like Rudy." She pointed at her brother. Rudy nervously smiled up at his teacher.

THE BULLDOZER looked from Alex to Rudy and back to Alex without saying a word. Slowly, the frown left the teacher's face. "Yes," she told Alex, "get them off the field. Good idea, Brackenbury." And without saying another word, she turned and marched back to the school building.

Alex let the rock that she had been holding fall to the ground in relief.

"Man, was that a close call!" Zack exclaimed.

"You're telling me," Aaron agreed.

"She didn't even ask you if you put those rocks in the field," Janie pointed out to Alex.

"Yeah, that was strange," Alex responded. "I kept expecting her to ask me more questions, but she didn't. I wonder why?"

"Maybe God is keeping you from getting into any more trouble," replied Janie.

Alex stared at her best friend. Janie hardly ever talked about God. But maybe she was right. Maybe God was keeping her out of trouble. "Thank You, Lord," Alex whispered to herself.

"Let's go home," Rudy whined. "My knee hurts."

When they reached Alex's house, Zack and Aaron helped the girls put together a soccer play that they could use against Joshua's team. The girls were excited. Even Janie was anxious to try it out the next day. If everything went right, the girls would score a goal all by themselves!

"This ought to show old smart-aleck Joshua Barton a thing or two," laughed Alex.

"I can hardly wait to see his face!" Janie added.

"Yeah," Lorraine agreed. She spoke shyly but her face showed just as much excitement as the others.

"Good," replied Aaron. "We are all set!"

"Watch out, Joshua Barton!" Janie cried and they all laughed.

"Are you ready? Let's play soccer," Ms. Springate called. She raised the whistle to her lips.

Alex grinned excitedly at Janie. She could tell that her best friend was nervous. "It's okay," Alex whispered. "When the whistle blows, just tap the ball forward to me and run to the left."

Janie nodded stiffly.

Alex glanced around at Lorraine. She had moved to the center of the field and stood a few feet behind Alex. She nodded at Alex to show that she was ready.

The whistle blew. Janie tapped the ball to Alex. Alex quickly rolled it back to Lorraine. The other team was caught off guard. They had expected the ball to move forward, not backward.

Before anyone could block her, Lorraine dribbled the ball to the right and shot it down the field to where Alex stood. Lorraine's kick was so powerful that Alex had trouble getting it under control. She was able to pass it sideways to Janie just as a guard from the other team rushed her.

Janie brought the ball under control and, before another guard could reach her, tapped it back to Alex.

Alex, now positioned in the top center of the goalie box, slammed the ball as hard as she could at the goal. WHAM! The whistle blew as Ms. Springate's arms went up. GOAL!

A cheer went up from Alex's teammates. Janie and Lorraine and Alex caught each other up in a three-way hug. Aaron ran downfield from his goalie box to help celebrate the goal. It took Ms. Springate a full five minutes to restore order to the soccer field.

The excitement carried through the entire game as Alex's team won, four to two. Lorraine had defended well, kicking several power kicks to the opposite end of the field. And Janie surprised everyone by scoring a goal when she kicked the ball between the goalkeeper's legs!

At lunch, the girls talked over the game. "Did you see Joshua's face?" one of them laughed.

"I thought he was going to bite holes in his

shirt when Janie scored the second goal," another one said.

"Me, too," Janie giggled. "He had his shirt in his mouth and chomped on it like this." She filled her cheeks with air and made rapid movements with her teeth.

"You look like a nervous chipmunk!" Alex said, choking on her laughter.

The girls laughed so hard that Mr. Carpenter had to come over to their table to quiet them down.

"Lorraine, you kicked some really good balls

out there," complimented one of the girls.

"Thank you," Lorraine replied.

"Yeah," another girl agreed. "How did you learn to kick a ball so far?"

"I have been practicing with Alex," answered Lorraine.

"Wow," the girls exclaimed. "Hey, Alex, can we practice with you, too?"

Alex laughed. "Well, I guess so. We always practice on the soccer field at the last recess."

"We'll be there!" the others promised.

Mr. Carpenter gave up trying to keep the girls quiet. He just smiled and winked at Alex and Lorraine.

CHAPTER 8

Ready! Aim! Fire!

"Did you get your invitation to Julie's slumber party?" Janie asked Alex excitedly.

"Yeah," Alex replied. "I found it in my mailbox last night."

"Me, too." Janie danced down the sidewalk. "I just love slumber parties!"

"Hey," Alex cried. "I wonder if Lorraine was invited?"

"Lorraine?" Janie exclaimed. "Alex! Can't you do anything without Lorraine?"

Alex stared at her best friend in surprise. "Sure I can," she told her. "I just wondered if Julie invited her. What's wrong with that?"

"Oh, nothing," Janie snapped, "if you don't count ignoring your friends and never having time to do anything at recess except practice soccer with Lorraine!"

"I was just trying to help her," Alex defended herself.

The two girls continued their walk to school. Neither spoke another word. Alex didn't know what to say to Janie. Maybe Janie was right. Maybe she was spending too much time with Lorraine. But Lorraine needed her friendship and God was counting on her to help Lorraine.

"I'm sorry, Janie," Alex said as they climbed the steps in front of the school building, "if I have spent too much time with Lorraine. But God wants me to help Lorraine and I have to do what He says."

Janie didn't answer. She just let out a big sigh.

As soon as Alex stepped into the classroom, Lorraine bounded over to her.

"Look what I got!" She proudly held up an invitation to Julie's party for Alex to see.

"Fantastic!" Alex cried. "Janie and I are going, too."

As soon as Alex could manage to talk to

Julie alone, she said, "That was really neat of you to invite Lorraine to your party."

Julie stared at Alex in surprise. "It wasn't so neat," she replied. "I only invited Lorraine because I thought you might not come if I didn't. You and Lorraine are such good pals these days!"

Alex was stunned. Were all of her friends angry with her because of Lorraine? Was she going to lose all of her friends? What about God? Did He know about all of this?

As soon as she got home from school, Alex told her mother what Julie had said and how Janie had been mad at her that morning.

"It's hard for your friends to understand why you have to spend so much time with Lorraine," Mother explained. "They don't see why it's important for you to help her."

"I have tried to explain it to Janie," Alex grumbled. "If she would just join me in helping Lorraine, then we could be together at the same time."

"But Janie doesn't see it that way," Mother told her. "Remember, Janie was not the one that God asked to help Lorraine."

"Yeah," Alex agreed glumly, "He asked me. Why did He have to ask me?"

Mother put her arm around Alex's shoulders and squeezed her tightly. "Maybe He asked you because He needed a person He could count on to do the job. You know, it is really an honor when God asks you to do something for Him."

"I guess so," Alex sighed. "But why does it have to be so hard?"

"Well, you know what I always say," Mother reminded her.

"I know, I know," Alex replied. "Whatever is worthwhile takes hard work." She imitated her mother's voice.

They both laughed.

"I'll be interested to see just what happens at that slumber party," Mother said, winking at Alex. "Maybe God has a few good surprises for you and Lorraine there."

The end of the week finally came. For Alex it had been a hard week. She had tried to divide her time equally between Janie and Lorraine. It seemed that the only thing she had accomplished was to hurt Lorraine's feelings by twice calling off her practice to play with Janie, and to make Janie mad by continuing to pay a lot of attention to Lorraine!

When Alex arrived at Julie's house, the other girls were already setting up a Monopoly game in the family room.

"Hey! Here's Alex!" someone cried.

"Come over here, Alex," Janie called. "We're going to play Monopoly. Do you want to play?"

"Sure," Alex replied. She waved at Lorraine who was sitting by herself in a corner. "Come over here, Lorraine, and play with us."

Lorraine's face brightened and she hurried over to sit beside Alex. Janie sat down on Alex's other side. Alex knew that Janie was annoyed with her for inviting Lorraine to play, but Alex just couldn't let Lorraine sit in a corner all night.

Later, Julie's parents came in to say good night and to tell the girls not to stay up too late.

"But, Mom," Julie complained, "you are

supposed to stay up all night at a slumber party. That's what they are for!"

Her parents laughed. "Just try to be quiet," her father suggested.

The girls decided to watch a movie. They spread their sleeping bags on the floor. As expected, Alex found herself between Janie and Lorraine.

About halfway through the movie, Alex noticed that most of the girls were asleep. The only ones awake were herself, Julie, and Lorraine.

"Hey, Julie," Alex whispered, "look at all these sleepyheads. Even Janie's asleep!"

"I am not asleep," Janie mumbled. "I just have my eyes closed."

"I know a good way to wake them up," Julie cried. She grabbed a shoe box from a shelf and motioned Alex to follow her into the kitchen. Lorraine and Janie came, too.

Alex gasped as she saw what was in the shoe box. Water guns! The box was full of them.

Julie began filling the kitchen sink with water. Alex grabbed a couple of guns and plunged them into the water. "Come on, let's fill 'em up," she urged.

After all the guns were filled, Alex, Lorraine, Janie, and Julie grabbed two apiece and tiptoed into the family room. They moved into position so that a water gun was pointed at each girl.

"READY! AIM! FIRE!" they cried.

"YEEAAAACK!" the girls on the floor cried as streams of cold water hit them full in the face.

Everyone began running around the room, shooting and dodging the water. Some of the others found the collection of water guns in the sink and began shooting back. The room became full of screaming, wet girls.

"QUIET!" roared a voice from the door.

Alex looked toward the door. Julie's father stood there, his face red with anger.

"Uh, hi, Dad," Julie squeaked.

"What is the meaning of this, Julie?" her father asked loudly. "Whoever heard of having a water gun fight in the family room? I would have expected this from a group of boys, but not from you girls!"

"Sorry, Dad, we got carried away," apologized Julie.

As it turned out, Julie had to get the hair dryer and several dry T-shirts for the girls. She promised her father there would be no more water gun fights.

"Brussels sprouts, your dad was sure mad," Alex said after Julie's father went back upstairs.

"We shouldn't have been so noisy," Janie observed.

"Hey, we better let the water out of the sink," Alex suggested.

"Oh, yeah." Julie reached under the water and pulled out the drain plug. Nothing happened. "Oh, great, the sink is clogged," Julie exclaimed.

"Probably from all that popcorn that we spilled," Alex replied. "Why don't you turn on the garbage disposal and get rid of the popcorn?"

"Good idea," Julie agreed and flipped a switch to the right of the sink.

Again nothing happened.

"Oh, no," Julie cried. "Now the disposal doesn't work. I'm really gonna get it for busting the sink."

"Take it easy, take it easy." Alex tried to calm Julie down. "Whenever our sink is clogged and our disposal doesn't work, my mom sticks a broom handle down the drain and taps it with a hammer and the disposal comes unstuck."

"Great, let's do it!" Julie ran for the broom and hammer. "Here." She handed them to Alex.

"Okay, here goes." Alex jammed the broom handle down into the drain. Then she hacked it with the hammer.

"It moved!" she cried triumphantly. "I felt it."

"Excellent!" Julie cried and flipped the switch to the garbage disposal before Alex could pull the broom handle out of the drain.

CRRUUNCH! The garbage disposal tried to grind up the broom handle.

"Quick! Turn it off! Turn it off!" Alex screamed.

Julie flipped the switch. The girls stared at one another in horror. "Now what am I going to do?" Julie moaned. She scowled at the broom stuck upside down in the kitchen sink.

"You could tie some ribbons around it and tell your mom it's a new decoration," kidded Janie.

"Very funny," frowned Julie.

"Well, help me get it out of there," said Alex. She and Julie climbed up on the sink, grabbed the broom and jerked. BAM! WHAP! Alex, Julie, and the broom tumbled to the floor.

"Hurrah!" their friends cheered.

"Your mother's really going to wonder who ate the end of her broom," Janie told Julie. "It looks like a giant mouse has been nibbling on it."

"Well, maybe she won't care too much," Julie said hopefully, "if I can get this sink fixed." She reached for the garbage disposal switch.

"Wait!" Alex grabbed Julie's hand before she could flip the switch. "First, let's see what's

in the drain before we turn it on again." Alex dug her hand down into the drain and made a terrible face. She dragged up a mound of soggy, squishy popcorn and a few wood chips from the broom.

"Ooooooh." The girls wrinkled their noses.

"I think I got it all," said Alex. "Try it again."

Julie flipped the switch. Nothing happened.

Julie covered her face with her hands and slid to the floor. "It's not fair," she groaned.

"I think you killed it," Janie said.

Alex tried flipping the switch on and off several times. Still nothing happened.

"My dad's gonna kill me," Julie wailed. "He'll never let me have a slumber party again!"

The other girls looked at each other helplessly.

Suddenly, Alex felt someone tap her shoulder.

"Alex," Lorraine whispered. "I think I know how to fix it."

"What?" Alex cried.

"What?" Janie hollered.

"What?" Julie exclaimed from the floor.

Lorraine blushed as all eyes turned on her. She gulped and repeated, "I think I know how to fix it."

Julie was up off the floor instantly. "Well, why didn't you say so? Come on, Lorraine, fix it," she pleaded.

Lorraine plopped down on her hands and knees and stuck her head inside the cabinet below the sink. Then she reached her hand inside and felt around for a bit. Finally, she pulled her hand out again and said to Julie, "Now try it."

Julie looked at Alex and shrugged. She flipped on the disposal switch. The garbage disposal began to hum and grind.

"You did it!" Julie grabbed Lorraine in a hug.

"Hurrah for Lorraine! She did it!" all the girls cheered.

"What did you do anyway?" Alex asked Lorraine when things had quieted down a bit.

"There's a reset button on the bottom of the disposal. I just pushed the button," Lorraine replied.

"Awesome!" Alex chuckled.

With sighs of relief, the girls trooped back to the family room. Alex passed around cans of cherry cola to celebrate Lorraine's victory over the garbage disposal.

"Lorraine, sit by me," someone cried.

"No, Lorraine, come sit over here," someone else called.

Alex grinned. Lorraine had suddenly become

a hero. Well, her mother had said that God might have some surprises at the slumber party. But a busted garbage disposal? Alex laughed out loud.

"What are you laughing at?" Janie asked.

"Oh, I'm just happy the way things turned out tonight," Alex smiled at her best friend. And she and Janie curled up on their sleeping bags beside each other to watch the end of the movie.

CHAPTER 9

Open House Mouse

"Hurry up, Alex, or we'll be late," Mother called.

"Okay, Mom," Alex hollered. She raced down the steps, two at a time. BAM! She hit the bottom of the stairs, causing the pictures on the hallway wall to rattle. T-Bone, who had been resting in the front hallway, woke up and began barking and whining.

"What's all the racket?" Father asked, coming into the hallway from the living room.

"Nothing," Mother replied with a sigh, "it's just Alex coming down the stairs."

"I should have known," Father teased and handed Alex her jacket from the hall closet.

"Rudy, come on! Open House starts in ten minutes!" This time Father called up the stairs.

A door slammed upstairs and Rudy bounded into sight. CLUNK! CLUNK! CLUNK! He, too, took two steps at a time. Rattle, rattle went the pictures. T-Bone, who had just settled down, jumped back up and barked.

Father and Mother laughed. "How many times have you two rehearsed that scene?" Father asked.

"Huh?" Rudy and Alex frowned.

"You both charged down the stairs the same way, causing all the pictures to rattle and T-Bone to bark. Your father wondered if you had planned it that way," explained Mother.

"Oh, no, we didn't," Alex told her father. "It just worked out that way."

"I see," chuckled Father. He held the front door open for them. The family was going to the Kingswood Elementary School open house. All except Barbara. She had said that she was much too old to attend such things. Alex was glad. Who wanted boring old Miss Mushy along anyway?

When they reached the school, the first room that they had to visit was the library.

"See, there it is!" Rudy shouted and pointed proudly at the giant pyramid display.

"My goodness!" exclaimed Mother, stretching her neck to see the top.

"I'm impressed," said Father. "How many boxes did you say it took to build it?" he asked Alex.

"It took us a week to stack 617 boxes," she answered her father. "But it only took Rudy thirty seconds to knock them all down!"

Father and Mother laughed. Rudy made a face.

Next they visited Rudy's classroom. THE BULLDOZER did not say a word to Alex although Alex kept expecting the teacher to mention the rocks in the soccer field. When they finally left, Alex breathed a sigh of relief.

Upon reaching Alex's classroom, Alex and her parents said hello to Mr. Carpenter. Alex then began showing Mother and Father around the room.

"Ho, ho, Firecracker, very good," said Father when he saw the many stars after her name on the running chart.

"Thanks," replied Alex modestly. "I hope in a few more days Lorraine will have her first star up there. She almost made it today."

"I'm sure she will," Mother encouraged.

"Where's Rudy?" Father suddenly asked, turning around to look for his son.

"Oh, he is over there," pointed Mother. "He is looking at some kind of a cage."

"That's our mice cage," Alex told her mother.

"Your what?" Mother exclaimed and wrinkled her nose.

"Our mice cage," Alex repeated. "We are raising white mice."

"Ooooh," Mother shivered while Father laughed.

Alex led her parents to a corner of the room where a giant map of England was being constructed. "See," Alex pointed. "I got to draw in the rivers and color the English Channel."

"Well, how nice . . ." Mother began—but suddenly a look of horror crossed her face. "AAAAAH!" she screamed. "THERE'S A MOUSE ON MY FOOT!"

Alex and Father looked at her in surprise. Mother shook her foot and something small and white dashed across the room.

"EEEEEK!" several ladies cried. They climbed up on chairs and desks to get away from the mouse. Alex's mother jumped on top of a table.

"GOBLIN!" Alex roared above the screams. "DID YOU LET THAT MOUSE OUT?"

Rudy gave Alex one of his guilty but innocent looks. It meant that Rudy had let the mouse out but that he hadn't meant to let the mouse out.

Father and Mr. Carpenter took turns diving under the desks to try and catch the mouse. Someone was smart enough to shut the classroom door so that the mouse could not escape down the hallway.

A few of the mothers continued to scream, especially whenever the mouse hid under the desk on which they were standing. Alex was glad that her mother was not the screaming type, although she did look rather silly standing on the table. If Alex had not been so worried about the mouse, she might have laughed.

Father and Mr. Carpenter could not seem to catch the mouse. They looked worn out and a little angry.

I bet Rudy gets it tonight, thought Alex. She glanced at her brother. He stood in a corner with his hands covering his mouth.

Finally, the mouse stopped running long enough for the men to barracade it in a corner. Mr. Carpenter lowered the cage down beside the mouse and the mouse ran into it.

"HURRAH!" everyone cheered.

Father and Mr. Carpenter smiled and congratulated each other. The ladies began laughing at themselves for being so afraid of the mouse.

Mr. Carpenter set the cage high on a shelf in the back of the room just so no one else could accidentally let any mice loose. Rudy had to apologize to Mr. Carpenter.

"Oh, that's okay, young man," chuckled Mr. Carpenter. "I will remember this Open House for the rest of my life."

"So will I," laughed Father.

"Me, too," agreed Mother.

"Well, leave it to a Brackenbury," hissed a voice in Alex's left ear.

Alex whirled around and met Joshua Barton's teasing eyes.

"It figures that your brother would be dumb enough to let a mouse out of its cage," he taunted.

Alex stared at Joshua for several seconds without saying anything in reply. Oh, she wanted to. She wanted to say something mean and ugly to Joshua. But she didn't. She kept her mouth firmly closed. Maybe it was because she was standing near her parents, and she wanted to look more grown up in their eyes. Or maybe she was more grown up. Whatever it was, Alex did not say anything mean or ugly. Instead, she waited until she knew her teacher and her parents were listening before replying to Joshua.

"Why, Joshua," she said with a sweet smile, "thank you for being so concerned about my brother, Rudy. I didn't know you cared."

"Huh!" Joshua frowned. He began to back away from Alex.

"Oh, don't leave, Joshua," Alex called after him. "I want to tell you what an absolutely gorgeous shirt you have on tonight!" And Alex began to walk toward Joshua, batting her eyelashes wildly as she had seen actresses do on television.

A frightened look came over Joshua's face. He turned and ran, tripping over people in his hurry to get away from Alex.

"Oh, Alex, that was so funny!" cried Janie

as she hurried up to her friend's side.

"I agree. That was the funniest thing I have ever seen," exclaimed Mother, wiping her eyes.

Alex laughed. Rudy laughed. Mr. Carpenter laughed. But no one laughed louder than Father. His booming laugh filled the room and echoed around it.

CHAPTER 10

Champions

The next morning Alex was still laughing at the look on Joshua Barton's face. As soon as she awoke, she remembered and giggled into her pillow.

Of course, Rudy had helped to make last night especially funny by letting the mouse escape in the classroom. Alex laughed loudly as she remembered her father and Mr. Carpenter on their hands and knees and her mother and the other ladies perched on tables and desks.

"What's so funny?" a deep voice asked from the doorway. Father stood there in his bathrobe and slippers.

"Oh, Dad," Alex gasped, "Wasn't last night the funniest night you have ever had?"

"Hmmpf," Father grunted. "Crawling

around on my hands and knees after a mouse that my son let out of a cage at open house is not exactly my idea of fun!" But before he walked back to his bedroom, he gave Alex a long wink.

Alex began to hum as she gathered together the clothes she was going to wear to school. Things were going well at school, too. It was hard to believe how fast Lorraine was improving in soccer. Why, she could kick the ball as hard and as far as Alex, herself, could kick it.

Alex smiled, remembering how, at yesterday's recess, Lorraine had demonstrated her kicking abilities for some of the other girls. And those girls had been impressed. Some had even asked Lorraine to practice kicking with them!

And the boys? The boys no longer groaned when it was Lorraine's turn to help defend the goal. Now they asked Lorraine to be a defender. It was great!

The only thing that Alex wished Lorraine would accomplish was to make her first mile. She had come close. She had missed it yesterday by only a few seconds. Maybe today would be the day.

When Alex reached school that morning, however, she quickly forgot about running. The story of the mouse escaping from its cage at open house the night before was quickly spreading through the classroom. Everyone was talking about it.

"I wish I had been here when it happened," one boy sighed.

"Yeah, we left too early," another complained.

"You should have seen how my mom leaped up on my desk," laughed someone else.

"My mom wouldn't have done that," another commented scornfully.

"Oh, yeah?"

Alex could not help smiling as she listened to the conversations around her. Rudy certainly had a way of making life more exciting.

Before Mr. Carpenter could start class, he had to explain how he and Alex's father had finally caught the mouse. The students had to inspect the mice in the cage to be sure that all were accounted for and that none were hurt.

"I'm so glad Rudy didn't let all six of them escape," Alex whispered to Janie when it was their turn to look inside the cage.

Janie giggled. "If he had, your dad and Mr. Carpenter might still be trying to catch them."

When Alex and the others went outside to run, Alex took off at a terrific speed. It was as if all the happiness and excitement inside of her were suddenly let loose. Her feet flew with joy. No one could catch up with her. Not even Joshua Barton.

"A new class record!" Mr. Carpenter yelled in Alex's ear as she finished her final lap. Alex grinned. Here was something else to make this day special.

"How is Lorraine doing?" Alex asked. She couldn't tell if Lorraine was on her first or second lap.

"She's on her second lap," Mr. Carpenter said.

Alex raised her eyebrows. Lorraine just might make it today. That would just make this day perfect.

"She has a good chance," Mr. Carpenter smiled. He, too, was rooting for Lorraine.

"COME ON, LORRAINE!" Alex screamed at the top of her lungs.

Janie, who had just finished running her mile, turned and cried, "HURRY UP, LORRAINE!"

Zack, standing near Alex, hollered, "LET'S GO, LORRAINE. YOU CAN DO IT!"

Then Aaron yelled, "RUN, LORRAINE, RUN!"

Before another minute had passed, everyone was cheering for Lorraine. The noise was so loud and so long that several teachers stepped outside to see what was going on. Ms. Springate hurried over to join the excitement.

Several children had dropped back to run with Lorraine as she completed her final lap. Alex stood next to Mr. Carpenter, her eyes glued to his watch.

"Oh, God, please let Lorraine make it," Alex silently prayed. She could hardly stand the excitement. Her eyes sparkled and her feet just wouldn't stop jumping.

"Ten, nine, eight . . ." Mr. Carpenter counted down.

"HURRY, LORRAINE!" Alex screeched and held out her arms as if to pull her friend across the imaginary finish line.

Lorraine crossed it with four seconds to spare. She fell into Alex's arms and the two girls hugged each other until the tears rolled down their cheeks.

"You are a champion, Lorraine—a real champion!" Alex cried and pounded Lorraine on the back.

"So are you, Alex," gasped Lorraine. "I couldn't have done it without you!"

The incredible joy that had been building inside of Alex all morning suddenly came alive causing her to leap high into the air. Raising her hands as high as she could, Alex reached toward the heavens.

"Thank You, Lord," she called to Him. "Thank You for helping Lorraine and me to run our race!"

Amen.